Sweet Dreams!

By Anjalee Jadav

Published by Blurb.com
Copyright @April 29, 2016

Chapter 1:
Save The Date

It's a typical day in summer of May 2015. In Maui, Hawaii. Dottie, a typical 21-year-old. Taking a vacation. She saved her money to go on this trip. Since she graduated from high school. She took time off before she decided to go into college. She wanted to be sure of which path to take. Before she majored in anything. Her mom advised her to take a break. And then decide. Because people go into college. And find out that the major they wanted was not what they wanted. Many people change their majors. And never complete anything. You have to be certain. Her mother would say.

Now Dottie is laying out on a beach, in Hawaii. She was enjoying the breeze and beautiful scenery. She was taking photos of different views, all day. Then Dottie said to herself. Maybe I'll become a Photographer. And become a storm chaser. While tasting the salty air, and hearing the waves of the ocean splashing against the shore. She was thinking to herself. This is the life.

Dottie, a server at Joe's Barbecue, in Denver Colorado. Saved all her tips and bought herself a plane ticket to Hawaii. Back at home she was considered very beautiful. She had brunette hair, light complexion, and brown eye's. She was 5.6 tall. And always had long hair. Taking a sip of a margarita. She hears some people playing frisbee. And all of a sudden. A frisbee landed on her lap. She almost spilled her margarita. Then some people were walking up to her to get their frisbee back. A girl said sorry. The wind blew the frisbee into a different direction. Dottie said. It's alright Dottie hands the frisbee back to the girl. And then the girl runs away.

Dottie then decides to go back to her hotel room. And get a bite to eat. So she rolls up her towel, packs up her beach tote, and finishes her margarita. She puts her glass in her tote bag, and walks up the beach. Sh heads towards her beach view room. It was a cozy room. With a king sized bed. It had a little tiki bar, and a sunk in tub in the bathroom. Dottie gets in the shower. And washes off the salt on her body. You'd be surprised that sand can get into the most darndest places. She washes her hair. And stands in the strea of water. The water was massaging her back. Then she shuts off the water. And gets out, dries off her body, and gets dressed. She puts on a Hula dress, wi flowers. And puts on her makeup. She blow dries her hair, and combs out her tangles.

Then she gets her purse. And pulls out her hotel key. She locks the door, and takes the elevator to the first floor. She walks into the hotel restaurant, The Tiki Room. Which had a bar, and someone playing the bongo drums. She gets seated. And some Hula girls were dancing on the dancing floor. They were encouraging people to join them. So they went around the tables and pulled people onto the dance floor.

Then the server came to her table. And asked what she wanted to drink. She said she would like an ice tea. And she was given a menu. She was eyeing the list of choices. She picked the Hawaiian Burger, with french fries.

As Dottie waited for her food. She checks her cell phone. She see's a text message from her ex-boyfriend. Please take me back. Can't stand a day without you. . She quickly puts her phone away. It's a little late for that. After catching him with Susan. She knew that it was over hen. And it is not going to change now. The waiter eturns, and puts her food down. She fixes her burger. And takes a bite. The juice from the meat was satisfying. t was delicious.

After Dottie was finished eating. She decides to see the sunset from the boardwalk. She pays the tab. And walks outside, onto the boardwalk. She pulls out her camera om her purse. And takes a picture of the beautiful pink unset against the ocean. Dottie thinks to herself. This is day she'll never forget. She takes out her journal and ocuments this day. As a day she'll tell her grandkids' someday. She was sure to save the date.

Chapter 2:
Trouble in Paradise

It was morning. Dottie had slept in until 10:00 am. She was cuddled in her hotel bed. And was really enjoying the morning sunshine through the window. She then gets out of her bed. And heads towards the bathroom. She was suggesting she start packing to go home tomorrow. She had bought herself some souvenirs last night while she was on the boardwalk. She bought some shell jewelry, and a shirt that said Aloha on it. She was trying to find room in her bags. Then she turned on the weather channel. To check the weather.

There was a warning of a tropical storm coming to Hawaii tonight. They were instructed to stay indoors. And plane travels were to be delayed. Great I get to stay longer!

Dottie exclaimed.

So, Dottie orders room service for breakfast. She ordered french toast, with bacon, orange juice, buttered croissant, and fruit.

She was getting dressed. When the room service came to her door. She opens the door. And there was a really cute Hawaiian clerk standing there. He wheeled the cart into her room. And set it by the window. She tipped him. And he said thank you Mam. Please call me Dottie. Mam makes me sound old. Okay, Dottie Miss. He leaves suddenly. And Dottie eats her breakfast.

The day went by, as Dottie was reading a novel from Lauren Conrad. It was about a girl trying to make it in L.A. She was reading on the porch of her hotel room, overlooking the ocean. She saw dark clouds moving in. And some lightning strikes in the sky. The wind was picking up. And was starting to howl. She quickly moves inside. And turns on the news. The tropical storm was supposed to be epic. It was claimed to have 50 mph. winds. And flood warnings were out. They said any tourists were to stay indoors. And avoid driving on the roads at all costs.

Then she heard a knock on her door. It was the maid. She asked if she wanted her sheets changed and turn her bed. And she had fresh towels for the bathroom. So, Dottie went to the first floor. To let the maid do her cleaning.

She went to the hotel shop indoors. She spotted a unique statue of a girl kneeling and holding a lotus flower. She checked the price. It was $30.00. It came with an inscription. It would bless her with fertility. The clerk then told her. Be careful with this one. It will grant her a child when the moon is blue and full. Dottie pays for the statue. And the clerk wrapped it in tissue paper.

Dottie left the shop to go back to her room. She took the elevator. And walked in the hallway of her floor. She unlocked her door, and went inside. She looked out the window, and it was raining like crazy.

The wind was howling, it sounded like trains racing.   The ocean tide rose and was splashing against the sand. Then all of a sudden the lights went out. The electric went out. Then she heard a knock on her door. It was the Hawaiian clerk. He had some candles to light her room. Dottie said thank you. And read his name tag, Danny. Danny left. And Dottie arranged the candles next to the window. She sat in a chair. Watching from indoors. She thought to herself. I wonder if the moon is blue and full tonight. The clouds were dark. And there was no moon visible. Dottie pulls out the statue. And unwrapped it. She admired the detailing it had. It came with a name. Luna the fertility goddess.

Chapter 3:
The Spell

Dottie woke up from thunder in the middle of the night. By this time the storm was crazy. And Dottie was scared. It sounded like ghosts howling. And she remembered that hotels usually had a few ghosts in them. So Dottie gets up. And lights some more candles. The electric was still out.

So, she puts on her robe. And goes into the hallway. And they had battery operated lamps to light. Then she saw the maid. And the maid was vacuuming the hallway.
She was humming to herself. Then she recognised Dottie staring at her. And she frowned. You should be asleep miss. There is nothing they can do. About the storm. So Dottie said. Sorry, the thunder woke me up and I can't sleep. So the maid said. Okay miss. But stay out of trouble.

Then Dottie heard the maid chant something. *Sweet Dreams my child. Fall into the magical lands. The lands that carry you through the wind. Sweet Dreams my child. And let Graham's tuck you in.*

Then Dottie all of a sudden, got really sleepy. And went back to bed in her room. That night. Dottie had a dream. She was on the beach. The ocean was calm, and soothing. It was sunny. And she was walking on the beach. She notices that half the sky was sunny. And half the sky was night. Then she noticed that the moon was blue and full. Then she saw someone. It was Danny. And he was smiling to her. He wanted to have her sit next to him on the beach. He hold's her hand. And kisses her cheek. He said Luna is very powerful. But she is good. He asked. Why did you buy the statue? When you were warned. She said. I liked the carving of it. It made her feel peaceful. Luna has that effect on people. But why the fertility goddess?

Dottie then said. I can't get pregnant. She had an infection that destroyed her ovaries. And was the real reason her and her ex boyfriend broke up. Her ex boyfriend wanted children. I was hoping the fertility goddess could heal me.
Danny then says. Let Luna hear you. She does bless people of your state. Then Danny disappeared.

And Dottie awoke. It was morning. And the storm left an overcast. It stopped raining. And Dottie looked out the window. The tide rose a whole 10 feet into the shore. And, finally the sun was peeping out of the clouds. It felt good to see the sunlight.

Then Dottie turns on the weather. And it said the tropical storm has moved to the Indian ocean. And was gone. They said any planes are safe to go to the United States.

So Dottie, calls the clerk to pick up her bags. To get a cab to the airport. Dottie kept the statue in her carry on. Along with her camera. Only this time. It wasn't Danny who came. It was an older man. And she was then directed down stairs. She called for a cab. And the clerk loaded the cab of her belongings. She checks for her plane ticket. And it was in her purse.

Now she was homebound. And reached the airport. There were employees sweeping the water from the terminal roads. And making the planes take off safely. She checks in at the airport. And goes through the metal detectors. It didn't beep. So she walked through. And picked up her belongings that would be carry on. She then goes to her terminal and waits for them to call them to board the plane.

Then the girl opened the doors. And called them to board the plane. Dottie waited for the handicapped to board first. And then she stood in line. She turned in her ticket, and boarded the plane.

As the plane took off. She said. Goodbye my beautiful Hawaii.

Chapter 4:
Home Sweet Home

The captain went on the speaker. And said the plane will soon be landing. Dottie was awakened by people fidgeting with their belongings. They were instructed to buckle their seat belts. So the light came on. Dottie buckled up. And the plane was circling the terminal roads. She landed in Denver airport.

Dottie, walked with her belongings out the terminal. And headed to the baggage claim. She then was greeted by her ex boyfriend Stephan. She said sharply. What are you doing here? Dottie, please take me back. Why should I? Dottie exclaimed. Because I can't live another day without you! Will you marry me? Are you crazy? Only crazy about you. And what about Susan? I caught you with Susan! Susan is not the woman I love. The woman I love is you!

Dottie didn't know what to do. She was dumbfounded. She said. Help me with my bags. So Stephan carried all her luggage. And put them in a limo. That he called. Dottie got in the Limo. And was expected to go home to her condo. But was surprised that they were headed a different direction.

Dottie said. Where are we going? Trust me. I want to show you something. Said Stephan. They were then taken to a jewelry store. And then Stephan got out of the limo. And escorted Dottie to the door. And Dottie was shocked. They went inside. And Stephan got down on his knee. And said will you marry me? You can pick any ring you want. Dottie was beyond excited.

Dottie picked out a princess cut diamond. It was a pink diamond. With little diamonds embroidering the outside.

So, Dottie said yes! I will marry you. Only if you say you can live without children. (Forgetting about the Luna statue). We can adopt. Stephan replied.

Dottie and Stephan kiss. And it was a kiss to remember. Welcome Home! Stephan whispered in her ear.

Chapter 5:
The Blue Moon

A month went by. And Dottie and Stephan were planning their wedding. Stephan moved in with her. And they were going over the wedding ceremony. I want a beach wedding. Dottie informed Stephan. Anything you want. You shall get.

As Dottie was dusting her statues. She came across Luna. She forgotten about Luna. And knew that they needed to wed on a Blue Moon. She told Stephan what the statue meant. And he was interested. Do you think Luna will heal you? He asked.

Dottie remembered her dream that stormy night. And said. I'm sure of it.

So they went online and googled the next Blue Moon. It said the next Blue Moon was on July 31st, of the year 2015.

So they set the wedding date. They will wed on the beach in Maui, Hawaii. On July 31st, 2015. They wanted a small wedding to be able to travel to. They only wanted their family and closest friends. Which narrowed the guest list, to about 50.

We don't have much time. Stephan said.

Tomorrow I go wedding dress shopping with my best friend Mary. Dottie had goose bumps just thinking about it.

Dottie was so excited. That she couldn't sleep. She woke up early morning. Her appointment was set at 10:00 am. She got breakfast. Eggs and toast, with orange juice.

Then finally after waiting to go. Mary came to the door. They carpool to the bridal shop. In Mary's car. Dottie didn't know what to look for. Then the sales rep. Greeted them. And said. Can I help you? Dottie said I'm the bride. And I don't know where to begin. Well what kinds of styles do you like? I like the sweetheart neck line, and I want lace, with a train. Answered Dottie.

So the sales rep searched through the racks. And picked out several options. The first one had too much ruffle. The second was better. More what she was looking for. But Mary said next. So Dottie pulled on the third dress. And Mary was smiling. This is the dress. It was a blush colored lace, sweetheart neck line, with a train. It fitted her like a glove. And was gorgeous!

Chapter 6:
Sweet Dreams

So as the days went by, of planning Dottie and Stephan's wedding. They booked their flight. They were packing their bags. And Dottie carefully packed her wedding dress in a hanging bag. So it wouldn't get wrinkled. She also put Luna in her carry on. Dottie had grown attached to Luna over the month. And included Luna in almost everything.

Then a week before the wedding. They make their flight. They still had planning on the other end of traveling. For their wedding. And had to book the spot on the beach. And they were sure that at least half of their guest list was attending. As the plane landed in the Hawaiian air port. They held hands. And got their belongings. Dottie was allowed to carry her wedding dress on the plane. She did not want to risk it getting lost in baggage claim.

They get into their limo. And go towards Turtle Bay Hotel. It was a different hotel, then the one, Dottie stayed at before. The room had a lovely view of the ocean. It was breath-taking. Dottie was taking pictures of Stephan and the scenery.

It was the night before the wedding. And Dottie had a dream. Luna came to her. And said. I am so happy for you. On the night of your wedding. You shall be cleansed and healed. You will be with child by sunrise of the next morning.

Dottie wakes up, refreshed. Stephan was in another room. For the superstition it's bad to see the bride before the wedding.

Then she heard a knock at the door. It was her mom and her best friend. They came to help Dottie get ready for the day.

Dottie's mom was lacing up her dress. And her best friend Mary was making her flower bouquet. Mary was a florist. And does exquisite work. Dottie looked like a princess. She was beyond excited. She was shaking. And her mom said. I felt the same way about marrying your father. I wish daddy could be here. He's watching right now. Wherever he is. His spirit is in your heart forever. Dottie teared up. Mary was doing the finishing touches of Dottie's make up. And Dottie looked in the mirror. She was a beautiful, princess, going to the ball. To marry her prince.

Chapter 7:
The Wedding Night

Dottie was walking down the aisle with her mom. She looked at the sky. The sun was setting, and she was looking for the Blue Moon. Then she noticed that the sun and moon were out at the same time. She knew that in India that means that there will be a wedding. And this was true.

She reaches the platform. And Stephan Foster was looking really good. He had his black tuxedo on. It was blue on the embroidery. He was smiling. And Dottie saw that he teared up a little. Then the pastor said. Ladies and gentleman, we are gathered here today. To witness Stephan Foster, and Dorothy Mayfair, in holy matrimony.

Then the pastor read them their vows. And they placed their rings on their ring fingers. They were holding hands. And the pastor said. We now welcome Stephan and Dorothy Foster. You may kiss the bride. They kiss. Just as the moon rose and was blue.

The reception was short. Because only 20 people came to their wedding. So they only had to reminisce to all the tables. Dottie was excited for the Honeymoon. It was the night.

She could be with child. So Stephan and Dottie left to go to their Honeymoon suite. Their was red rose petals scattered on the king sized bed. It was turned down. And it was a sight of elegance and beauty. Stephan and Dottie had a night to remember. By morning Stephan was still sleeping. But Dottie was up and she took Luna The Fertility Goddess statue out of her bag. And said thank you for a magical night. Dottie knew it was too soon to know if she was surely was pregnant. But she documented this date in her journal. It was a night to remember. It was the second date she will tell to her grandchildren someday.

The End!

Epilogue:

Dottie was rocking in a rocking chair. Holding her little baby girl. She had just given birth to her first child. She named her Anna Marie Foster. Anna was cuddled in her arms and was asleep. Dottie knew that she was blessed. And that Luna granted her wish to be a mother.

Dottie, also is a student to be a fertility specialist. She will help women become pregnant. When they are struggling to get pregnant. She was certain, and had many Sweet Dreams.

About the Author:

Anjalee Jadav, lives in the desert of Arizona. She has a dog and a cat. And enjoys her days with family and friends. She loves to write stories and articles.

Anjalee, is also a gifted artist. And has her very own art gallery online! To access it go to:
http://anjaleeartgallery.spruz.com

Lightning Source UK Ltd.
Milton Keynes UK
UKRC011356290519
343423UK00013B/188